For Viktor. The story of Mussorgsky's 'Pictures at an Exhibition'.

By Robert Philip Bolton

Best read with the playing of 'Pictures at an Exhibition' (original piano version) by Modest Mussorgsky (1839-1881).

Also by Robert Philip Bolton
Jacko. One Bloke. One Year.
The Boys and Men of Auckland's Mickey Rooney Gang
The Fine Art of Kindness
Six Murders?
To The White Gate
Underneath the Arclight
My Marian Year
The Boltons of The Little Boltons
The Tapu Garden of Eden
The Collected Short Stories (in which is combined *Nana's Special Day and other stories, The Dolphin and other stories,* and *Quickies.*)

Robert Philip Bolton is a dedicated music lover. He was born in New Zealand in 1945. He has been writing fiction most of his adult life. Most of his work is about New Zealand and New Zealanders. He lives in Auckland.

For Viktor.
The story of Mussorgsky's 'Pictures at an Exhibition'.
By Robert Philip Bolton

robert@bolton.co.nz
ISBN: 978-0-473-13125-8
Cover design: DIYpublishing.co.nz

Author's introduction

All music lovers seem to know and at least appreciate, if not love, Mussorgsky's *Pictures at an Exhibition.* As one of those who learned to love the suite early in life, especially the original piano version — so raw and edgy and 'Russian' compared with Ravel's oh-so-French orchestration of 1922 — I was always surprised and disappointed to read the mini-abstracts describing the pictures (and thus the music) usually included on album covers. Compared with the vitality of the music they seemed so vacuous and, from album to album, so much the same as if copied from a single and somewhat inaccurate source.

This short book is designed to put things right. It was written to honour Mussorgsky and his *Pictures* which itself was written by Mussorgsky to describe the posthumous exhibition of pictures by his friend Viktor Hartman and thereby memorialize his friend's life and work. In this he certainly succeeded: without Mussorgsky's *Pictures* it is doubtful if history would remember Viktor Hartman at all.

The book is written in Mussorgsky's voice as he guides a young companion around the exhibition. If read to the accompaniment of the original piano version of *Pictures* the reader will find that the duration of each narrative section — including each of the promenades — if spoken aloud, or read slowly if silently, is about the same duration as the musical piece it describes. Indeed, important events in the narrative often intersect with appropriate moments in the music although I have not been driven to achieve this at the expense of the overall effect.

There is an introduction to cover Mussorgsky's meeting of his fictitious friend outside the exhibition hall — the hall of the Academy of Artists in Saint Petersburg — and a conclusion which ends the story with Mussorgsky and his friend going to meet others at the Maly Yaroslavets, the composer's favourite bar.

* * * * ** * * * * * * * * *

Viktor Alexandrovich Hartman was born in 1834. He died of an aneurism which came suddenly, in the street, while walking with Mussorgsky, in 1873; he was just thirty-nine years old. Mussorgsky had met and befriended him only in 1870 but he loved him passionately (how Hartman felt about Mussorgsky is not known) and was deeply moved by his friend's sudden death.

Hartman had led a comfortable, untroubled existence. He was a genre-painter, designer, illustrator and architect, one of several artists Mussorgsky used as a model for creativity. Unlike Mussorgsky, who had never travelled beyond the Russian borders, Hartman was widely travelled and worldly-wise. But while he was loved and admired by his friends it seems that he was merely a competent artist.

For the six months or so after Hartman's death Mussorgsky was preoccupied with his opera *Boris Godunov* which had had its triumphant premiere in January 1874. Meanwhile he was collaborating with Count Paul Suzor, president of the Architects' Society, and Vladimir Stasov, an influential Hartman promoter, whom Mussorgsky called Généralissime due to his influence over many young artists, in the mounting of a large exhibition of Hartman's work. The exhibition, in the Hall of the Academy of Artists in Saint Petersburg, opened during the second week of February, 1874, and ran until March.

It is not known exactly when or how often Mussorgsky visited the completed exhibition although one assumes from the intimacy he felt with the pictures, and the quality of his compositions which results, that he made many visits. The manuscript shows that he finished *Pictures at an Exhibition* only three months later. The final page is dated 22 June, 1874, while the dedication to Stasov is dated 27 June, 1874. It was dated ready for printing on 26 July.

* * * * ** * * * * * * * * *

Modest Petrovich Mussorgsky was born on the sixteenth of March, 1839, in Karevo, near Pskov. He had a happy childhood on a sleepy rural estate with all the pleasures of nature, a nanny, private tutors and music teachers. Following his family's wishes he entered the army in 1856 but left, unhappy and disillusioned with the dissipated life of an officer of the guards, only two years later. In the meantime he had joined a group of young composers in Saint Petersburg later known as The Five and led by Mily Balakirev who urged Russian composers to stress their national heritage.

History tells us that Mussorgsky was a highly intellectual, impressionable, stubborn, lonely, musical genius who was undoubtedly frustrated by the absence in Russia, at that time, of any musical theory to support his techniques and experiments. And for most of his life he was poor. The indulged, semi-aristocratic lifestyle of his childhood and youth was destroyed forever, in March, 1861, by the Emancipation Proclamation of the new Tsar Alexander II. Under this proclamation large landowners were required to turn over their holdings to local peasants. This changed Mussorgsky's life and led to his poverty, degradation and alcoholism. He died, on the night of his forty-second birthday, in 1881.

Note that all dates are from the Julian calendar, used in Russia at that time, which lagged twelve days behind the Gregorian calendar used in the west.

Arriving at the hall

Ah. You are here already. I hope you have not been waiting long. It is very cold. Look at the black sky. Soon it will snow again, I think. And then the ice. Such a climate we have. And yet I know no other so I do not mind. But, come, it will be warm inside the Academy.

Oh, yes. Thank you, my young friend. Poor Viktor. After seven months my heart still aches. He was only thirty-nine. I was with him not long before, you know. In the street. He took ill. I didn't understand how bad it was. He stopped. Leaned against a wall and turned pale.

I asked him, so calmly, so naively: 'What's happening, Vityushka?'

'I can't breathe,' he gasped.

And all I said was: 'Rest a bit, my dear friend, before we continue.'

That's all. Such a fool. But I didn't know. I had no experience. No expectation. Men killed in battle; yes. To be gored by an ox; yes. To fall from a hay-stack or be thrown from a horse; yes. To drown in the Neva; of course. But to die so young from nothing.

An aneurysm they said. So sudden. Such waste. He was so clever. Not a genius you understand — I know I *said* he was genius but that was for publicity — but very clever. So versatile. So many ideas. So much potential. And *such* a man.

But now he is gone. He lies, even now, in the frozen earth, to be soon forgotten. But the world should know what *might* have been. All the world should know about dear Viktor Alexandrovich.

Give me your things now. Your coat and hat and scarf and gloves. We leave them here.

(Thank you, madam.)

Now. Have you been here before? No?

It is very elegant. An honour for Viktor.

We go through this door directly into the great hall.

Inside the hall

Promenade 1.

Look around. And ahead. Such a tribute don't you think? Hundreds of pieces — and more to come — to show his amazing versatility. But do not stop yet. Walk on with me. There is so much to see but so little time.

I shall show you my favourites. You can come back later if you wish. Such an effort to show it all. Mostly the work of Généralissime. He pushed us. Spurred us on. And, of course, the Count. His influence with the Academy. It could not have been done without him.

I helped with advice because I knew so much about Viktor. Indeed, we inspired each other, he and I. And he confided in me, and I in him, and we both in Stasov.

I know I walk crookedly. It is the price of my obsessions. The food of course. Rich tastes acquired in childhood. A country estate. A loving mother. A spoiling nanny. Private tutors. But now, impoverished by the proclamation, cast off my land,

I am an urban peasant, as gross as the peasantry, so people stare at the way I walk.

But you are here and I care not what people think. My clothes are clean; my hair and beard are trimmed. I promenade with you proudly, for the sake of Viktor Alexandrovich, to introduce you to him, to converse with him again, and to show you my favourites.

Stop here. This one. Number two-hundred-and-thirty-nine in the catalogue.

Look carefully. What do you see? What do you hear?

Gnomus.

Latin for 'Gnome'.

A bent and shrunken and deformed and grotesque creature. With crooked legs too short, and feet too deformed, to properly carry its bulky trunk. Look at the distorted head. The gaping mouth for the nuts. The thick and matted hair under the hat. And, under the thick fringe, eyes so round and red and rolling and wild and — yes — insane.

It is truly ugly and bizarre. And yet there is much in the little hulk that is strangely beautiful. It *was* made, you know. And it *did* work. Fashioned in wood to hang on the Artists' Club's Christmas tree. That was — let me think — yes, in sixty-nine; just four years ago this Christmas past. I didn't know Viktor then. I knew his reputation, of course, and we met just a few weeks later. But I remember the ugly little gnome very well, hanging from the tree by its neck. The nut went in here — in the mouth — and then, by a system of leverage, it was cracked with ease.

But what a fantastic drawing of a fantastic human-like creature it is. It jumps out at you, does it not, Viktor's gnome? Like Glinka's sorcerer *Ruslan,* or my own village idiot. I see it here, but I *hear* it here — in my mind — stumbling through life with sudden, jerky and uncontrollable spasms, its face a twisted grimace. It clenches its bony fingers into a fist which it shakes at the world with anger and frustration. Then it comes, drooling, wheedling, with false and disgusting charm, pleading, while yet full of fear and dread. It is so ashamed of being a freak. It hates its own body, and yet its shrivelled brain cannot think to plot its own ending and thereby end its own suffering.

So it, the horrible ugly and suffering little creature, is doomed. And I am doomed to look at it, eternally still and bizarre and black on the creamy paper, but, in my mind, forever twitching and jerking uncontrollably, and leaping about on its short legs, waving its ungainly arms, opening its disproportioned mouth, showing its yellowed teeth, and, lacking a true voice, expelling only dreadful and unearthly sounds.

Every time I see it I hear in my mind such terrible crying and moaning — like the sounds of souls burning in hell — that I go to bed haunted by its unspeakably evil noises. When, I wonder, will they leave me alone?

Look at it. So disturbing and yet so beautiful that I cannot turn away my eyes.

Promenade 2.

But, come. We must continue. No, no. Not these. The gnome has upset me. Walk ahead to something more benign.

You ask so I shall tell you. I speak so little only because I do not force my opinions. I love to talk but I do not enjoy trivia or gossip. And of my work I speak only to myself, consulting nobody.

Your other question? Karevo. A small town near Pskov. My father was Pyotr Alexeyevich. He was a bastard but his father, who came from ancient gentry, brought him into his family and gave him his name. I had three brothers born before me but the first two died of the pox before the age of two. My dear mother, broken-hearted, superstitious, and wary of the names of saintly martyrs and their burden of death — she had lost two infants remember — named me—

But, wait. The castle. We are here.

Il vecchio castello.

Italian for 'The Old Castle'.

Stand back now. Is this not a grand picture? So big, yes, but not for the sake of size. Viktor — he was an architect first — was trying to capture the nobility of this castle showing that its beauty was embodied in its purpose.

Nothing, he said to me, pointing at the castle, is here for nothing. He said that everything — every stone — had been carefully placed for a purpose. That is why he so carefully defined each of the great blocks here at its base. And to emphasize their imposing size — and the great height of the walls — he has put people here: the serenading troubadour, and the young women with their baskets of flowers and fruit.

See how handsomely the castle's smooth rising walls are crowned by overhanging battlements, with merlons and embrasures of such ideal proportions they appear, so sharply defined against the sky, to have been cut — no, sculpted — by an artist. Their proportions please the eye so easily, Viktor believed, because they serve their purpose so well.

Viktor said that the castle was designed and built in the middle ages. He said one of the Roman popes sheltered here during the political wars of the

Renaissance, and it was old even then. But now, he said, it sits in ruins on this great bluff, above this vast valley, in a climate so kind and pleasant that Viktor said that I, used only to the north, not knowing the south at all, could hardly imagine it.

But old and broken there, in southern Italy — Sicily perhaps — he has rebuilt it anew here, in the painting. He has replaced every loose and crumbled stone — coloured them all fresh and new — and rebuilt the portcullis with stout new timbers reinforced with newly-forged iron.

And see how, below, in the valley, he has pictured the patterns of today's vineyards and olive groves, villages and estates, all washed by a warm autumn sun casting soft and gentle shadows. The scene is a romantic vision — the product of his imagination — but the grandeur of the castle is portrayed with accuracy and truth.

See how the blue sky and white clouds contrast with the dull yellow-greyness of the castle walls. See how the artist touches the brush delicately to the rough canvas — look closely — to make us believe that *this* is a tumbling stream, *this* its companion road, *this* a bridge, *this* an avenue of yellow poplars leading to *this* important villa and its outbuildings, *this* a white horse, *this* a tent flying a flag, and *this* a gathering of country people at a vegetable market. There are even, *here*, children playing with a black yapping dog.

But, sadly, above them all, an unhappy serenade fills the air and slips down the hill into the vastness of the valley. Here, on the grassy slope at the base of the castle wall, we see the travelling troubadour in his blue and orange suit, strumming his little lute and singing his mournful melody.

Listen to his song. It has a southern rhythm, monotonous and relentless. But the air is so sweet and melancholy that it makes me weep with both sadness and joy.

These young women have left their work to stop and listen. They are enchanted by what they hear. They sway together slowly, holding their baskets on their hips, watching him intently with their black eyes.

Is he singing to one of them? All of them? They hope, but I think not. The song's poignancy means he is singing to someone far away. Someone who cannot hear. Even so, he is compelled to waft his song, again and again, into the warm air hoping it will drift, accidentally or by fate, into the right ears.

Sometimes he glances up, hopefully, to the top of the castle walls, to the lofty tower. But then, seeing nobody there, he casts his eyes down again to the earth, then briefly to the fret-board to check his fingering, and then — still playing and singing — he lifts his head slowly and gazes across the valley with unfocused eyes. Perhaps he hopes his love will materialize from the hazy atmosphere.

How beautiful tragedy can be.

How sweet it can sound.

But then, suddenly, as if he realizes the futility of his song, he slashes the strings of the lute — loudly and rudely — and walks away from his little group of admirers.

Promenade 3.

Now. A short walk to the next piece.

Oh, yes. My dear mother named my older brother Filaret. You see: *not* a saint's name. And for me a Latin name that means what it says: Modest. Humble. Unassuming. A good choice I think. It was the twenty-first of March in our calendar, eighteen-thirty-nine. I am almost thirty-five years old.

Poor Viktor. This year he would have turned forty.

Tuileries. (Dispute d'enfants après jeux.)

French for 'Tuileries. (Dispute between children at play.)'

But here we are. He painted the Tuileries gardens in Paris so well. In the summer I think.

Ah, you have been there. You are fortunate.

The public have shown their approval of the beautiful scene but for me the fascination lies *here*, in the children playing beside the path. I hear them so clearly, running and skipping and chasing and giggling. Their nurse is here, you see, sitting in the shade, looking on.

Do you like children? Oh, my friend, they fascinate me. They understand me. And I them.

And then the big girls hide behind the statue. From the little one. And from nanny.

'Where are you?' calls the little boy, alone and afraid.

'Don't tease Etienne,' calls the nurse to the girls whom she cannot see.

Then. Out they jump. Boo! They startle him.

'You were alone,' chant the girls. 'You couldn't find us. You were afraid.'

And the little heir runs to nanny. Crying and ashamed.

That's another thing I understand about little ones.

They can be so cruel.

Bydlo.

Polish for 'Cattle'.

And look. Here. Hitting us right between the eyes: the black-and-brown gloom of Sandomierz. I always imagined it just as Viktor has painted it: a dark, threatening and unfriendly place full of stupid people. An entire race of oafs as dense-headed as their *bydlo*. Heavily yoked to their dull, repetitive and unrewarding work, dragging themselves through life, day after day, forever pulling the heavy load that is their heritage; a nation and people devoid of culture and incapable of uplifting thoughts.

Alas, life can be dreary and tiresome for everyone — I have had my share of hardship — but how terrible to be born naturally stupid in an enslaved country. A nation of people so stupid that if you are not a Catholic then you are a Jew. What a cursed choice.

This is how I see and hear them, my young friend: as plodding oxen. Heavily muscled in neck, shoulder and limb, leaning into the bulky yoke, slow and dim-witted, hauling they-know-not-what they-know-not-where for they-know-not-whom. Seeing through dulled eyes, in drooped heads, but understanding nothing. They do not step and prance like steeds. Instead, these pitiful Polish cattle, they plod ponderously across the brown and muddy landscape under a perpetually grey sky.

Do you hear, as I do, their weary lumbering tread as they drag themselves from their work? There is a cart, with makeshift sides, made of rough timbers bleached white and split by rain and time. And instead of slender shafts running forward to a willing pair there is a log anchored to the yoke with iron bolts and rusty chains. Massive wooden wheels, with crude wooden spokes, bump roughly over the stony ground. And the whole contraption sways awkwardly with the clumsy movements of the *bydlo*.

They labour up the last small hill to their disgusting hovels. There, unwashed and unfed, they will lie for the night in their working rags, on filthy beds, and sleep the sleep that comes to exhausted beasts of burden.

Thank God to be not Polish.

Thank God, my friend, to be Russian.

Promenade 4.

Now. Something more pretty.

Let me take your arm. I know. People tell me: 'You are looking old and fat, Musoryanin,' they say. 'You must take more care.' But the friends I made at college; their loyalty has cursed me. They are brothers, and they do the same work for me, but one is cheap and the other expensive. They have been with me so long I cannot now be without them. Now, after so many years, they have corrupted my organs and yet I cannot turn them away. So, my over-indulgence — in food and drink and, yes, I know, the other of which we shall not speak — brings illness and disease.

But I care not.

Balet nevylupivshikhsya ptentsov.

Russian for 'The ballet of the unhatched chicks'.

But look at this. *This* is what I care for: the beauty and innocence of Russian children. You see, Viktor designed the costumes for *Trilbi* at the Maryinski. The girls and boys from the theatre school played the little canaries breaking out of their shells. Listen to them pecking so lightly. Then, suddenly, one cracks the delicate shell and breaks out with a joyful peep.

Do you remember *Trilbi*? The ballet? Perhaps you were too young. But do not these drawings — designs for the costume maker — their little beaks, their feet, do they not show Viktor's cleverness and versatility? Ah! Another is out.

More than ever I want to write down what I hear in Viktor's work. You know, I have written music for a magpie, a goat, a beetle, a drake, a mosquito with a bedbug, a screech owl and a parrot; so perhaps I shall picture the canary chicks pecking on their shells from the inside.

Look at the downy feathers of their neck. And can you not see them hopping about on the stage in Viktor's clever costumes?

And now, I hear them again. See the act of creation. A little chick at the moment of birth? Will he be a perfect roller? Now he is out. He makes his own little peep.

Then the last is out.

And it is over.

"Samuel" Goldenberg und "Schmuÿle".

Yiddish.

And immediately — just two paces away — together, *here*, we meet the Israelites. This one — looking so rich and dignified — I call 'Samuel Goldenberg'. My own joke. Look at his fine suit and his fur hat; not a *yarmulka* but an expensive hand-made hat. He looks out with confidence and a sense of superiority based, I venture, on a warm bed and a full stomach. I hear him with my heavy left hand. He speaks slowly, clearly and precisely, in deep rich tones. He pauses for breath. Then speaks again. His voice is powerful but not pleasant. It sounds ugly and cruel even to his own kind.

Look at the other. Such a contrast. In my mind I have named him 'Schmuÿle'. Another joke, but I detest Yiddish. You would too if you knew Deutsch as I do. This wretch — poor and without hope, don't you agree? — I hear with my light right hand in triplet tremolos to suggest his high voice and chattering teeth; his whimpering, snivelling prattle. He is begging from Goldenberg. His back is bent but he shuffles along, looking up at his rich neighbour through rheumy eyes.

But the rich man, feeling nothing but contempt, refuses. He dismisses him, but the beggar, with nothing to lose, will not be deterred. He thrusts a hand, filthy and callused, into Goldenberg's beard. They are both Jews, sharing the same ghetto as they share the same blood, religion, history and guilt. But they are also human beings which means they have their own poor who are despised by their own rich.

Viktor's wife was a Pole. From Sandomierz. He went there in sixty-eight and ventured into the ghetto to make these studies.

They are very evocative. I know because I have mixed with Petersburg Jews. I have listened to their songs. They are ancient and Oriental — not like our songs at all — and it is a challenge to find their slippery grey notes when the choice is only black or white.

I intend, one day, to go to their holy services but I must find a Jew who will take me. I *must* understand their music better.

Promenade 5.

Walk on. Walk on. These — all — are beautiful and important but my legs and feet ache, time is short, and I have friends to meet at the Maly Yaroslavets. Do you know it? It is very good, on Morskaya Prospekt, just across the river, near the place where dear Viktor had his turn. If only I had known. If only I had acted in some way — I know not how — he might have lived. They say not but I cannot help thinking it; feeling it. But — yes — you should come. You will enjoy the company; people like you and me who believe in Russia and things Russian.

It is good for me there. I confess I have been lonely since Viktor died. But I continued to work and now, as you know, *Boris* has been launched with great success and people want to meet me again, and buy me food and drink, and seek my opinion.

It has also been good for me to see the exhibition with you. I have had my secret thoughts about Viktor's pictures but today you have made me express my thoughts in words. Then — whether or not you have been listening — the spoken words have left my mouth and laid themselves down on the keyboard, in their proper order, in my mind, waiting only to be played. And I *will* play them. And when I have proven them worthy I shall write them down in Viktor's honour.

There is nothing I can do better in memory of my dear friend.

Limoges le marché. (La grande nouvelle.)

French for 'The Limoges Market. (The big news.)'

Stop here. Look. Not at the cathedral but at the people.

The chattering women in the market. Is not this scene exactly as you imagine a French market? Viktor told me he loved Limoges for its architecture — in the exhibition there are seventy-five drawings and paintings from there — but I like this one. For the atmosphere. Look. See *here*. Just a smudge of brown, I know, but I imagine it is a cow. And beside her is a farmer — I call him Monsieur Pimpant de Panta-Pantaléon — who thought his valuable cow, *Fugitive*, to be lost and is now announcing *la grande nouvelle* — the big news — that she is found. But the good wives of Limoges are not interested in *this* little incident because, *here*, by the fountain, Madame de Remboursac has acquired some fine porcelain dentures. And *this* man is troubled by his red nose.

* * * * * * * * * * * * * * * * *

Oh, how women everywhere can chatter and gossip quickly and loudly about anything to anyone not noticing that no one is listening to anyone but themselves so impressed are they with the importance of their own opinions. Meanwhile the poor people of the countryside, who set off for Limoges so early, with their fruits and vegetables, olives and mushrooms, goats and rabbits, and chickens and cheese, must stand and wait patiently, hands on hips, while the ladies of the town make up their minds about nothing more than a handful of nuts or a bunch of cheap spring onions.

Catacombae (Sepulcrum romanum).

The catacombs of Paris — in fact caves resulting from the extraction of the stone used to build the city — were filled with human remains taken from the city's cemeteries by Napoleon III's builders in the process of glorifying the city's architecture and landscape.

And now. Oh, misery. One pace to the left. Not Limoges. Not colour. Not life. But old Paris and dreadful death.

The cold catacombs. Underground passages, leading nowhere, as dark as death itself.

Here, in the cool and airless blackness, where nothing lives, not even worms and maggots, have cold lifeless bodies, shrunken and stiff, their putrid fluids seeping from their ruptured skin and natural holes, been laid — for how long I know not — until their soft guts soak into the stone, and their flesh falls away and turns to the same dust that is all about. Oh, what fear I feel and hear when I see Viktor's awful watercolour.

A guide — what kind of man can he be? — stands, in coat and hat, holding his lamp loosely at the level of his knees. It washes a yellow light on the rough walls, and on the sad cross — making soft shadows of Viktor and his friend — and brightly onto the flagged floor where it is least needed, and along the caged rows of black-eyed skulls with smooth and shining brows.

Who were these people? And what ghoulish person — when, why, in what mood, and by what light — fashioned the neat pigeonholed-cabinets, like those at the post office, and fixed them straight in rows. And then, separating so many skulls from their unconnected bones, callously brushing away dried skin and stiff hair, set only the hollow heads in neat rows looking forever across a black aisle to rows of matching cabinets and matching staring skulls, until someone, like Viktor, comes, I know not why, to look at such horror as we can hardly imagine.

I have met death much, but the meetings were not my choice. I would *never* venture, as Viktor did, into such a narrow and airless tomb merely to look eternity in the face ten-thousand times. It is, to me, like ten-thousand nightmares dreamed for ten-thousand nights by ten thousand cold and hungry orphans.

It is terror and dread beyond measure.

Con mortuis in lingua mortua.

Mussorgsky was fluent in French and German but, as he suspected, the Latin for 'With the dead in a dead language'. is not quite right: 'Con' should be 'Cum'.

Oh, my young friend, hold my arm. Your youth and warmth remind me of life.

But look. Oh it is horrible. Can you see? Step back. Step back more. More.

Now! See what happens? Not the living people — they are incidental — but the skulls. Viktor has led me to the skulls again and again. He has invoked whatever humanity remains, lingering like wisps in their bony structure, and so they begin to glow. Do you not see? It comes from behind the paint. From within the paper and through the paint. But it is more than light and pigment. It is — I don't know — but it happens every time and it is most eerie.

My Latin is weak but I feel them speaking. *'Con mortuis in lingua mortua.'* Is that correct? 'With the dead in a dead language'? It matters not. But if only it were possible. To speak with the dead. My darling cousin. My dear mother. Viktor Alexandrovich of course.

But it is a fantasy. A nonsense. I have no tolerance of faith and religion, and an afterlife in paradise. They who once lived are now dead and gone to nothingness. But sometimes, despite my belief, I hear the departed ones in my head. They chant a strange and ominous lament, continuously and unnaturally. It haunts me often. Stays with me. Like a companion sitting in the shadows at the back of the room, away from the window, humming a tuneless tune, waiting for me to finish my duties.

I hear the song even now. Feel it. See it. It waits only to be stroked from the box. A trill. A tremolo. What a cursed dirge it is. Perhaps it will leave me when I have written it down. Yes. I shall write it down as soon as I get home — later, when you and I have drunk our fill — and then the world will be haunted by it as I have been. And then, perhaps, the world will understand.

Wait now, and be quiet, before we move on. I need to calm myself.

Izbushka na kur'ikh nozhkakh (Baba-Yaga).

Russian for 'The hut on hen's legs (Baba-Yaga)'.

Now, at last, I feel better. Although this one, too, is very strange.

It is a clock designed as a little house on the legs of a chicken. A walking house.

Yes. Of course. It is Baba-Yaga's hut designed by Viktor as a clock. But I ignore the clock and see instead the wicked witch herself as she wheels through the air. See her flying low through the woods, between the trees, crouched in her flying mortar, peering over its rim, her coarse white hair streaming straightly behind her as she propels herself with the pestle. Now, out of the forest, she turns, without effort, soars high into the air, into the very clouds, turns again and swoops down past us — here on the ground — laughing and screeching evilly as only a witch can, before disappearing magically back into the dank and scented darkness of her forest home where her hut on legs awaits her command.

Did you have a nurse as a child? A nanny? Then you must have heard the tale of Baba-Yaga many times, just as I and Viktor did. Because Russian nannies share a love of Slavic tales of witches and giants and heroes, and the tale of their Baba-Yaga is one of the best: how she lives in the forest in a hut — something like Viktor's design I suppose — which stands on fowl's legs and can turn to face approaching visitors; and walk towards them; and chase them. Thus are hapless children, wandering innocently in the cool forest, looking for woodland flowers, juicy berries or summer butterflies, captured and murdered and eaten by the evil Baba-Yaga who uses her giant pestle and flying mortar to grind their bones to dust. Such a frightening story for little children who live in the country near a forest as I once did.

See here, in the catalogue, Stasov has written: *'Baba-Yaga's hut on fowl's legs. Clock, Russian style of the fourteenth century. Bronze and enamel.'* A poor attempt, I think, to capture the spirit of Viktor's design. It would, I agree, make an interesting clock. But it remains unmade, only a design on paper, and only the design of a clock. Fussy and ornamental and childish and not to my liking. I imagine Baba-Yaga herself. And I hear music for her that is lean — stripped of all embellishment — and shall write it so. But — and you have helped me today in giving my thoughts a better form — I shall acknowledge Viktor's design with a metronome mark of ticking clockwork.

You see, now, at Baba-Yaga's command, her fabulous hut stands off the ground, on its own straight legs, and sets forth, stalking through the forest on spread toes, scaly and clawed, turning to look this way and that through the woods, seeking the goodness and innocence which Baba-Yaga hates and lives to destroy. Alas, today, two or three more pure and simple Russian children will become victims of Baba-Yaga's evil. And tomorrow they will be added to the grim toll that makes the tale of Baba-Yaga more terrifying with every passing generation. Meanwhile they scream with fear and pain while she laughs with evil pleasure.

I hear it all. Even the key: *C major.* Baba-Yaga's hut. Baba-Yaga herself flying forth. Manoeuvring through the forest-scented air like a bird of prey — screeching like one — with a viciously-hooked beak made for nothing but ripping and tearing tender flesh. Then dashing back into the cool shade of the forest. Back to her magic house.

Bogatyrskie vorota (vo stol'nom gorode vo Kieve).

Russian for 'The knight's gate (in the ancient capital, Kiev)'.

But now, for a true architectural masterpiece, there, on the wall beside you. Not a curiosity to entertain children but Viktor's fitting tribute to Imperial Russia. It is the knight's gate. And can you hear the procession — such pageantry — passing through its majestical arches?

See the *konvoi* from the Caucasus. Quiet and alert, they walk rather than march. Their black eyes, under their bearskin hats, dart about seeking assassins. Their ungloved hands are gripped on their sheathed scimitars that wait slenderly within the scabbard, curved and pointed and sharp, ruthlessly ready for their lethal purpose.

Ahead of the royal carriage are the horse guards in their white ceremonial dress, their black boots flaring from their thighs, the royal eagle on their breasts, their helmets glinting rosily in the pale light. And, behind, the imperial guard, the *Semeonovski* regiment — not mine — looking rigidly ahead, marching mechanically on unbending legs, sweeping one fist up to the chest, and down again, slowly with deliberate precision.

This splendid gate was designed by Hartman to be built in Kiev. He was taking part in a competition of architects to replace the ruined gate and thus honour our beloved Alexander who, just eight years ago, survived an attempted assassination. But, alas, the competition was abandoned, and what would have been a striking monument was never built. Look at it. So grand and stately, it would have served as a solid expression of all that makes Russia different and better.

Now I hear the bells peeling joyously, up and down the scale so quickly that the hammers must strike sharply again and again while the bell-iron is still quivering resoundingly from the strike before. They are coming for a royal baptism. Oh what a parade it is. I hear the tsar himself, and the tsarina and tsarevich, and even little Nicholas, the six-year-old princeling who will himself be tsar one day. The child in the imperial carriage waves to his people, and they wave back at him and at the whole procession, laughing with pure happiness and pride.

Look at Viktor's gate. Surely it — he — would have won the prize. See how the columns seem sunk into the earth as though weighted down with old age; as though built at the very dawn of Russian history. That is what Stasov saw and I am inclined to agree with him. See how there is a pattern in the walls made by arranging differently-coloured bricks; and how the corner bricks are especially decorated with ancient Russian motifs and symbols. And see how the intricate wrought-iron-work at the sides is designed to lighten and the heavy appearance of the columns.

Then look up, at the belfry, the bells, and, above, the tall cupola in the shape of an ancient and traditional Slavonic helmet. It, my young friend, represents the *men* of Russia. And here, over the main arch, surmounted by the imperial eagle, is the intricate wooden fretwork, fashioned in a lace pattern — so very folk Russian — that shapes a *kokoshnik* and so represents the *women-folk* of our country. They stand together in this great gate, symbolically, the brave men and women of Russia, at the entrance to the ancient capital, defying the world, defending the city and the country, and yet welcoming any who come in peace with the inscription *'Blessed is he that cometh in the name of the Lord'*.

They are in the chapel of Saint Michael, whose figure appears on the shield above the main archway, and they are singing with such reverence and humility that it moves even me to bend my head. Such holy beauty, in so few human voices, as they sing the sacred Russian hymn, *'As you are baptized in Christ'*.

The human voice is the perfect instrument, and it is my vocation to hear it, understand it, and represent it. And the hymn represents all that is good and pure about our popeless religion, and about Vladimir's mass baptism of his people so long ago. If you cannot hear it now, in your imagination, you will hear it when I write it out and play it for you and the others.

Regard, once again, before we leave, the marvellous design of this gate. See it as a grand entrance to a beautiful city; an imposing symbol that embodies many other symbols that together represent all that is good about our people, our nation, our language and our religion. It is a solid expression of mother Russia, designed by a patriot, built in Russian stone, and planted deep into Russian soil.

Come now. We are finished. It is time for us to meet my friends. Indeed, you shall be my guest. I have the success of *Boris* to celebrate and, now, in my mind, a completely new piece unlike anything else ever written. Because thanks to you — because your presence has forced me to give words to my thoughts — I have almost written the gate's music in my mind. It will be full of imperial pageantry tempered by reverence for the holy sacrament of baptism using the baptized royal infant to symbolize the re-birth of the Russian people.

After you, my friend.

Leaving the hall

(Thank you, Madame. Yes. It is very cold outside. And dark of course. This is, however, the nature of our dear city in winter. But soon my friend and I shall be warm again thanks to another good friend — the friend of all Russians — whom we are about to meet.

Goodbye, Madame. We call a cab.)

You know, my friend, I must tell you plainly — before vodka and brandy and conversation cloud my mind, and I am already very tired — that, until today, representing some of dear Viktor's pictures at the exhibition has been only a vague plan. But now, with your presence forcing me to explain my thoughts, my plan is fully formed and I intend to start work immediately.

When? Well, it is now — what? — the end of February? Because it is so complete in my mind — even the intermezzos, the keys, the tempos, the pedals — I think it will take me a mere twenty days or so; as much as I need to write it out neatly for the printer. Providing, of course, that the brothers leave me alone.

My music will be clean and spare and strong. Piano music for a pianist to love. Music to make me famous in Russia. Music to make Russia famous in the world.

And I shall do it for Viktor to ensure that he, too, will be famous, and that his work will *never* be forgotten.

- THE END -